Parents and Caregivers,

Stone Arch Readers are designed to provide enjoyable reading experiences, as well as opportunities to develop vocabulary, literacy skills, and comprehension. Here are a few ways to support your beginning reader:

• Talk with your child about the ideas addressed in the story.

• Discuss each illustration, mentioning the characters, where they are, and what they are doing.

• Read with expression, pointing to each word. You may want to read the whole story through and then revisit parts of the story to ensure that the meanings of words or phrases are understood.

• Talk about why the character did what he or she did and what your child would do in that situation.

• Help your child connect with characters and events in the story.

Remember, reading with your child should be fun, not forced. Each moment spent reading with your child is a priceless investment in his or her literacy life.

Gail Saunders-Smith, Ph.D.

Stone Arch Readers

are published by Stone Arch Books
a Capstone Imprint
1710 Roe Crest Drive
North Mankato, Minnesota 56003
www.capstonepub.com

Library of Congress Cataloging-in-Publication Data
Yasuda, Anita.
The missing trumpet / by Anita Yasuda ; illustrated by Steve Harpster.
p. cm. -- (Stone Arch readers: Dino detectives)
Summary: Cory the Corythosaurus is excited about playing in the
school concert, but when the morning arrives his trumpet
is missing--and it is up to the Dino Detectives
to solve the mystery of who took it.
ISBN 978-1-4342-4155-9 (library binding) -- ISBN 978-1-4342-4832-9 (pbk.)
1. Dinosaurs--Juvenile fiction. 2. Brothers and sisters--Juvenile fiction. [1. Dinosaurs--Fiction.
2. Brothers and sisters--Fiction. 3. Mystery and detective stories.] I. Harpster, Steve, ill. II. Title.
PZ7.Y2124Mis 2013
813.6--dc23
                                        2012027053

Reading Consultants:
Gail Saunders-Smith, Ph.D.
Melinda Melton Crow, M.Ed.
Laurie K. Holland, Media Specialist

Designer: Russell Griesmer

Printed in the United States of America in Stevens Point, Wisconsin.
092012
006937WZS13

The Missing Trumpet

by **Anita Yasuda**
illustrated by **Steve Harpster**

STONE ARCH BOOKS
a capstone imprint

Meet the Dino Detectives!

Dot the Diplodocus

Sara the Triceratops

Cory the Corythosaurus

Ty the T. rex

The school concert is Friday. All
the dinosaurs are in the concert.

"I can't wait!" Cory says.

"I love playing my trumpet!"

Cory practices every day. He plays before breakfast. He plays on his way to school.

He plays after dinner. He even plays in bed!

On Friday, Cory wakes up
early. He practices some more.

Then he gets dressed and eats
breakfast.

"I'm ready!" he says.

But when Cory goes back to his room, his trumpet is missing. The trumpet case is empty!

"Oh no!" Cory says. "Where is my trumpet?"

Cory runs to his sister's room.

"Have you seen my trumpet?"
he asks.

"My dolls love music," she says.
"Ask them."

"Dolls don't talk," Cory says.

Cory's friends are ready to go.

"Come on," Sara says. "The concert starts soon."

"I won't be in the concert,"
Cory says. "My trumpet is
missing!"

"We'll find it," Dot says. "That's what Dino Detectives do!"

Sara looks under Cory's bed.

"It's not here," she says. "But
I found your missing socks."

Dot looks in the fridge.

"It's not here," Dot says. "But this pizza looks good!"

Ty looks in the trash.

"It's not here," Ty says. "But I
could use this for an invention!"

The dinosaurs look all over the
house. They can't find the trumpet.

"I guess I won't be in the concert," Cory says.

"Wait. Do you hear that noise?"
asks Cory. "Follow me!"

The dinosaurs run upstairs.

They see Cory's sister playing
the trumpet.

"My trumpet!" Cory says.

"My dolls wanted a concert, too!" his sister says.

"We will play for them after school," Cory says. "But I need my trumpet now.

"Hurry up! We don't want to miss the concert," Dot says.

"Let's go make great music!"
Cory says.

STORY WORDS

detectives	concert	practices
dinosaurs	trumpet	invention

Total Word Count: 292